P█████N BOOKS

F████Y WITCH AND THE THUNDER
█D

F████ ███itch is round and tiny and has a nose like a potato.
█████ ████ore, she looks as though she's been made out of
patchwork and straw. She lives in a ramshackle old house which
she sh███res with a variety of animals including her hairy old dog,
Casse███le. Fanny Witch is the village school teacher and all the
█hildr██ love her, even though she can get into some scrapes!

█n *Fa███y Witch and the Thunder Lizard*, Fanny conjures up a
brontos████urus to show the children exactly what it looked like,
██ut the ████rontosaurus starts wreaking havoc in the village and
██hen s███s Fanny Witch's Spell Book so she can't undo her
█agic! ████here is another monster at large in *Fanny Witch and the
████osnatch*. The Boosnatch snatches children from their homes.
████nny W████tch comes to the rescue and finds that the Boosnatch
█ just a ████ce and friendly, but lonely, giant.

████y St████ong is a teacher and lives with his wife and two
████████ Kent.

25p

Fanny Witch and the Thunder Lizard

Jeremy Strong

Illustrated by Annabel Spenceley

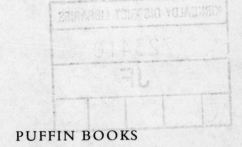
PUFFIN BOOKS

PUFFIN BOOKS

Published by the Penguin Group
Penguin Books Ltd, 27 Wrights Lane, London w8 5tz, England
Viking Penguin, a division of Penguin Books USA Inc.
375 Hudson Street, New York, New York 10014, USA
Penguin Books Australia Ltd, Ringwood, Victoria, Australia
Penguin Books Canada Ltd, 2801 John Street, Markham, Ontario, Canada l3r 1b4
Penguin Books (NZ) Ltd, 182–190 Wairau Road, Auckland 10, New Zealand

Penguin Books Ltd, Registered Offices: Harmondsworth, Middlesex, England

Fanny Witch and the Thunder Lizard first published
by Hodder and Stoughton Children's Books 1987
Fanny Witch and the Boosnatch first published
by Hodder and Stoughton Children's Books 1985
Published in Puffin Books in one volume 1989
10 9 8 7 6 5 4 3

Text copyright © Jeremy Strong, 1987, 1985, 1989
Illustrations copyright © Annabel Spenceley, 1987, 1985, 1989
All rights reserved

Printed in England by Clays Ltd, St Ives plc

Contents

*Fanny Witch
and the
Thunder Lizard*

Fanny Witch was round and tiny and had
a nose like a potato. What is more, she
looked as if she had been made out of
patchwork and straw. Her hat was as bent
as an old bed-spring and her dress so
worn out that even the patches had
patches.

Her ramshackle house was in no better state. The roof leaked and there were holes in some of the windows, but Fanny did not mind because she shared her house with a large and unusual family. There were several mice, a few rabbits, a family of squirrels, some rats, two badgers and some foxes, beetles, spiders and owls. There were swallows under the roof and a heron in the chimney pot, not to mention Fanny's hairy old dog, Casserole.

That was the way Fanny Witch liked it, with the animals popping in and out, day and night. 'Otherwise I would be lonely, wouldn't I?' Fanny would tell surprised visitors.

The house was next to the village
school, and Fanny looked after that too.
She was a rather forgetful kind of teacher
and often did not know whether it was
Sunday morning, Wednesday afternoon
or Tuesday lunchtime. In fact she
sometimes forgot about lunch altogether
and then the children would have to
remind her.

The village children were fond of Fanny. She was never cross if a fieldmouse decided to chew up a maths book to make a nest, or the magpies stole all the counting cubes because they liked the bright colours. And because she was a witch the children never knew what might happen next.

One Monday morning, when they were all sitting in their classroom, Jessica was reading a book about animals that lived long ago. There were pictures of all sorts of dinosaurs, but the one that fascinated her the most was the brontosaurus. She showed it to Max.

'That was the heaviest creature that ever lived on earth,' she explained. Max examined the book.

'How big was it?' he asked.

'It was bigger than the biggest truck you can think of.'

'I can think of a bigger truck than a brontosaurus,' claimed Max. 'I bet the brontosaurus wasn't as big as the truck I'm thinking of. Anyway, it doesn't look very big. It's got a titchy head.'

Jessica was reading the writing underneath the picture to see if it said exactly how large the bronto was, but the only other thing the book told her was that the word 'brontosaurus' meant 'thunder lizard'. She showed the book to Fanny Witch, and asked her why the ancient dinosaur was called a thunder lizard. Fanny smiled.

'Look at those legs, Jessica. They're thicker than tree trunks. If you went stamping round on legs like that you'd be called Thunder Jessy.'

Jessica thought for a moment. 'I don't think I'd like legs like that. Max says the brontosaurus was only titchy.'

Fanny Witch looked across at Max, who was now busy drawing the most enormous truck carrying six brontos, just to prove how small they were. Fanny took the book from Jessica and studied the picture closely. Then she pushed back her chair and got up.

'Well, I think perhaps we had better
have a little demonstration. Then Max
can see how big the bronto really was,
and you can see – and probably hear! –
why it was called thunder lizard. Come
on, children, out into the playground. And
you, Casserole, you can come too. I'm
just going to fetch something from the
house.'

The children went outside, with
Casserole running rings round them
excitedly, wondering why playtime was
an hour early. When Fanny came back
from the little cottage the children all
began whispering loudly to each other,
because under her arm Fanny was
carrying a very large and thick book, and
they knew at once that it was her Book of
Spells.

Fanny spread out the book on the playground and opened it up. The pages were brown and old and several spiders hurried out from between them as Fanny searched for the right place. Then she put Jessica's animal book next to it and pulled out her little wand. 'Jessica has found a picture of one of the largest land animals that ever lived. The picture isn't very clear so now we are going to look at a real one, but only for a minute or two because I don't want any accidents to happen. Stand back, everyone!' Fanny waved her wand. 'Ikky spikky spoo!'

A great cloud of brown smoke boiled up from Jessica's book, growing larger and larger and larger. There was a rushing, growling noise as the smoke slowly drifted away on the wind and there, standing in the playground, arching her enormously long neck and tapping the tip of her enormously long tail on the ground, was a fully-grown, very-much-alive brontosaurus.

Casserole gave a half-hearted woof and scampered behind Fanny's stripy stockings, only allowing his trembling nose to poke out between her legs.

'There,' said Fanny, matter-of-factly. 'That's a brontosaurus – the thunder lizard. She's quite big, isn't she?'

Fanny was very pleased at the way her spell had taken effect. As for Bronto, she stared slowly round at everyone with her tiny eyes. She looked startled, as if she were wondering what she was doing standing in a school playground on a

Monday morning, with half a dozen
children staring back at her, their eyes just
about falling out of their heads in
amazement.

There should have been more than six
children, of course, but eight of them had
run back into school to take shelter.
(Casserole was the first inside!)

'Don't be alarmed,' said Fanny.
'Bronto is quite harmless you know.'

Max eyed the dinosaur warily. 'Won't she eat us?'

'Of course not! She's a vegetarian – a herbivore. She only eats plants. Look – she's just swallowed the lilac bush.'

Bronto was having a nice quiet munch. There were bits of bush hanging out of the side of her mouth, and the children could hear a great deal of chewing and crunching.

'She's like a giant cow,' said Danny. Little Jo shook her head.

'My dad's got lots of cows but I don't think he would want one of those in his cowshed. It wouldn't fit.'

'It is VERY big,' said Max, who now seemed to accept that brontosauruses were staggeringly large.

At this moment the beast swivelled her little head round and stared at the small humans so far below. Slowly her long neck stretched out and she sniffed the air. Nearer and nearer came the head and a huge brown tongue flopped out like a bit of old face-flannel, all wet and speckled.

The children backed away.

'She's quite safe,' said Fanny with a smile. 'There's no need to . . . Hey! That's my hat you've got!'

Chomp, chomp, chomp – the old black hat vanished down Bronto's long throat, while Fanny ran round in circles, far below. She shouted and waved and jumped. Casserole was so upset at seeing the hat disappear like this that he dashed out from the school, charged round Bronto in one wild, noisy circle and

galloped back indoors again with all his hair standing on end.

As if in answer to all this, Bronto lifted her head to the sky and uttered such a bellow that it sounded like a train rushing through a tunnel. The school windows rattled and the six brave children still out in the playground took to their heels and raced inside. Now Bronto stretched out her neck once again and this time picked up between her teeth Fanny Witch's Book of Spells.

There she stood in the centre of the playground with the most valuable book in the village stuck in her ancient, leathery jaws, looking just as if she was off to the nearest library to change it for something better – probably something tastier.

Fanny Witch was beside herself. 'You can't! You can't! Put my book down at once! You can't eat that!' Bronto bellowed again, but with her mouth full of spell book it didn't sound so terrifying this time. She started to move her legs for the first time. One huge foot went up and came crashing down. Then another, and at each step the playground shook, dust rose in clouds and tiles slid off the school roof and crashed to the ground.

Bronto turned away and began to creak off into the countryside, her giant belly swinging from side to side. Fanny ran after her with a cry of dismay and grabbed the dragging tail. 'Come back, you book stealer! You monster! Come back here!' But the dinosaur only swished her tail.

Fanny Witch had to cling on for her life. She was whisked this way and that, through the air, until at last she could hold on no longer. With a startled yell she let go and went flying through the air with her patchwork dress flapping round her head and her multi-coloured stockings waving wildly. Down she came – splash! – straight into the school pond.

'Oh!' sighed Fanny, struggling out.

Dripping wet and trailing water weed from her head like a strange new hair style, she collapsed on the grass and stared out over the countryside, hunched up and miserable. Bronto could still be heard crashing away, but she was no longer to be seen. 'Now what am I going to do?' moaned Fanny, as the children crept out from the school to see if she was all right. 'What AM I going to do?'

By now half the village had come hurrying down to the school to see what was going on. The earthquake shuffle of the thunder lizard had caused all sorts of damage in the village itself. Plates had fallen off tables, jugs had spilt and one poor old grandad had fallen right out of bed. The children were quick to tell their parents all about the brontosaurus.

'She was gi-normous!' cried Max.
'As big as a whale . . .'
'As big as TWO whales!'
'Legs like tree-trunks . . .'
'And the biggest toe-nails in the world!'
Some of the villagers smiled. They were used to Fanny's spells. Danny's dad said: 'Never mind. All you have to do is say the Undoing Magic and the brontosaurus will go back into the book.'

Fanny got to her feet slowly, shaking her head. 'Oh dear, oh dear. Don't you see? That monster has eaten my Book of Spells. Eaten it! I have no idea how to make any Undoing Magic without my book.' Fanny looked from one face to another as with mounting horror the villagers realised what she was saying.

'Do you mean the brontosaurus is here for ever? In our village?'

Fanny nodded, and little drips of pond water trickled off her nose. A frog croaked and jumped out of one pocket and back into the pond. A stunned silence settled on the villagers, and from far away came the distant thunder of giant footsteps.

At length Little Jo's father suggested they made a trap for the dinosaur. 'We can't stand here doing nothing while that walking earthquake destroys our village. We could get a huge net and tangle the creature up.' But nobody knew where there was a net large enough to catch a brontosaurus.

Then Katie's mother had an idea. 'What about that big barn of yours? Suppose we got Bronto in there? We could shut the doors and she'd be trapped.' This suggestion immediately had everybody talking excitedly. They hurried over to the barn and had a look. It was certainly a very large building, and they decided that the brontosaurus would just fit inside.

Little Jo's dad fetched his tractor and a trailer and they filled the trailer with cabbages, because Fanny Witch said she thought Bronto would like cabbages a lot more than lilac bushes. They drove out of the village and down the valley, with

Casserole sitting on top of the cabbage
pile and the wind playing with his ears.

There was Bronto, wandering round
the edge of the wood. The tractor stopped
and Fanny and the farmer started to throw
cabbages at the dinosaur, until she lifted
her head, sniffed and gazed dreamily in
their direction.

Casserole leapt from the trailer and
barked furiously at the huge creature.
Bronto bellowed back, lowered her head,
and made a short charge at the dog. With
a squeal of terror Casserole turned tail and
fled into the wood. Fanny Witch was too
busy to call him back.

'Yoo-hoo! Look at these lovely
cabbages. Come on, this way!' The little
witch began to lay a trail of vegetables as
Bronto slowly but surely followed. Little
Jo's dad drove back towards the barn with
Bronto lurching along behind the tractor,
chomping up the cabbages.

At last they reached the barn and Fanny
Witch threw the last cabbages into the
back of the building. Then she and the
farmer hid behind the big doors and

waited. Along came Bronto – chomp, chomp, chomp. (By this time all the other villagers had hidden in their houses. It was the first time they had actually seen the monster.)

Outside the barn, Bronto paused. She poked in her head and thoughtfully ate a single cabbage. She went in a little farther and ate another. Then she took two creaking steps and ate a third, and five minutes later she was right inside the barn.

'Now!' yelled Little Jo's dad, and the doors were slammed shut and a great wooden bar put across the outside.

'There!' Fanny said. 'We've done it!' And she shook hands with the farmer.

At that moment the whole barn began
to creak and groan. Fanny rushed round
to the back. Bronto had thrust her head
out through a little window. She was
struggling to get right out and the barn
heaved and shuddered. The old timbers
creaked and squeaked as the building
started to lean heavily to one side.

Suddenly, with a great crack of splintering timber, the barn was torn from the ground and off went Bronto once more, wearing the barn like a badly-made overcoat. Her head and neck stuck out at one end and at the other her tail trailed behind, leaving a deep, wriggly mark in the dust.

The poor farmer now felt as upset as
Fanny Witch when she had lost her Book
of Spells, and could only sit down with
his head in his hands.

'Oh dear, oh dear,' sighed the little
witch. 'I have caused a lot of trouble.'

Bronto was now having a good explore
of the village. She was obviously still
hungry and didn't seem to mind what she
ate. She poked her pea-brained head over
Danny's garden fence and ate up all the
washing on the line: four pairs of socks,
Danny's football kit, three shirts, six pairs
of underpants, a vest and the best
tablecloth. Then the monster stuck her
head into Katie's bedroom next door and
gobbled up her new curtains.

By this time her swishing tail had
knocked down Danny's fence, and Katie's
goldfish were swimming round and
round an enormous foot that had
suddenly stepped right in their little pond.

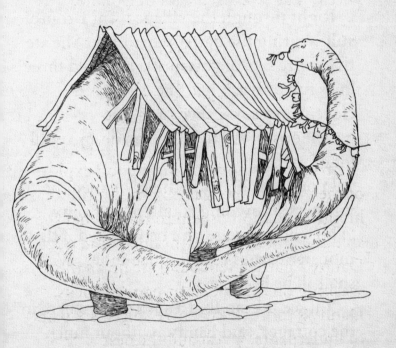

Katie's mum rushed out of the house
waving a broom.

'Go away, you big oaf. Leave my curtains alone!' Bronto lowered her head and mooed. Katie's mum gave a strangled scream and ran back into the house, but not before Bronto had grabbed the broom and eaten it.

Right through the village went Bronto, still wearing the barn on her back. She ate five more sets of curtains, a rug, and three lines full of washing. She destroyed eleven fences, six sheds and two greenhouses. All in all she made an awful lot of mess.

'You must do something!' wailed the villagers, crowding round poor Fanny. 'The whole village will be wrecked if that monster barges round much more. We shall all be homeless.'

'I'll see if I can find a spell somewhere in the cottage,' said Fanny, without much hope, and she hurried off to her tumbledown house, muttering over and over again: 'Oh dear, oh dear . . .'

Inside the house she searched and searched. She looked under cushions and on top of cupboards. She lifted up the sleeping fox on the armchair and looked beneath her. She crawled under the table where the chickens liked to go, but there was nothing at all. The only thing she found was her second best witch's hat, even more bent and battered than the first. Fanny stuck it on her head and sighed.

She was just about to give up the search
when there was a tremendous woofing
and barking. Casserole came racing into
the house with his tail wagging like a
windscreen wiper and his eyes shining.
He tugged hard at Fanny's dress. (She had
to put another patch on that spot later,
because Casserole's teeth went right
through!)

'What is the matter with you? What do you want?'

The dog barked, then tugged, then barked and tugged again.

'You want to show me something, is that it?' Fanny said to him. 'I hope it's not a bone, Casserole. It had better be something important.'

The dog jumped down and scampered away to the back of the school, with Fanny hurrying behind. Casserole kept looking back and barking. Right across the playground he went, out over the grass and into the woods.

'I do hope there's a good reason for this,' puffed Fanny.

At last Casserole stopped in a patch of long grass. He raised his hairy nose and howled, until Fanny came panting up to him. And then she saw what all the fuss was about. There in the grass, with a small yellow snail crawling across the cover, was Fanny's Book of Spells.

Fanny threw herself at Casserole and
hugged him madly, while he tried to
wash her ears as clean as he possibly could
with his long tongue. 'You are a
wonder-dog, Casserole! Come on – there
is no time to be lost.' Fanny tucked the
book under her arm and hurried back to
the village, with Casserole trotting
proudly at her heels.

When they reached the school they discovered that Bronto had somehow managed to leave the overcoat-barn in the middle of the High Street, and was now playing a loud ding-dong game with the school bell, hitting it with her nose. The villagers and the children were watching from a safe distance, and wondering what was going to happen next.

Fanny Witch marched into the playground, an enormous smile on her round face. 'Look what Casserole has found!' she cried. 'That daft beast didn't eat my Book of Spells after all, so now I can make the Undoing Magic.'

Fanny opened the book and bent over it, turning the pages one by one. She frowned, went back to the beginning and started again. Then she stopped and looked at the middle of the book closely. 'Oh,' she murmured. 'Bronto seems to have eaten the very page I wanted. What a nuisance.'

At this point Bronto got tired of ringing the school bell and she lumbered into the playground to see what was going on. 'I'd better find a spell quickly,' said Fanny, hastily turning the pages. Bronto gave a grunt, bent down and carefully whipped Fanny's second best witch's hat from her head. Chomp, chomp, chomp. It was gone. 'Thank you very much!' cried the witch. 'That was my next best hat. Well, I've found the spell for you!'

Bronto stared back at Fanny with an I-don't-care-one-bit expression on her face, and Fanny's hat sticking out of her mouth like a giant smashed up cigar.

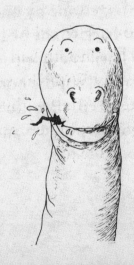

Fanny pulled out her little wand,
glanced at the book and cried: 'Ikky
spikky spoo!' A noise like a cannon
exploded over the playground; there was
a blinding flash, then silence. The
villagers stared at Bronto and slowly crept
out into the open. Fanny smiled and shut
her book with a bang that made the little
yellow snail drop off and hurry away.

And Bronto, the dinosaur, the
thunder lizard, stared back at nothing.
She didn't move. Her tail had stopped
swishing and her mouth had stopped
chomping. Fanny Witch had turned her to
stone, just like a statue, with half Fanny's
hat still sticking out of her mouth. That
was turned to stone too.

Casserole barked and barked and it
sounded more like laughter than anything
else. The children ran over to the monster
and began climbing all over the tail and
sliding down it with great whoops of
delight. The villagers stared and stared
and then they laughed and clapped, and
last of all they cheered Fanny Witch.

Fanny Witch went bright red with embarrassment. Then she picked up her Book of Spells and went right round the village waving her wand and crying 'Ikky spikky spoo!' wherever Bronto had caused damage. The barn was suddenly back in the right place. The fences and sheds and greenhouses were made as good as new. Even the clothes lines and curtains came back, but Fanny got a bit muddled over those and Danny found himself with a new ballet dress instead of a football kit.

But nobody minded one bit because the biggest monster in the world was not a big monster any longer. She had become the biggest climbing frame and the longest slide and the best thing the children had seen in their playground ever. As Jessica slid down the tail and landed with a bump at Fanny's feet, the little witch said quietly: 'Jessy – if ever I suggest turning a picture dinosaur into a real one again, you will stop me, won't you?' Jessica laughed, but Casserole tugged at her dress and growled very loudly. He wouldn't let her forget.

Fanny Witch
and the Boosnatch

Fanny Witch was short and dumpy and
she had a nose like a big potato. She
always wore a tall black hat. It was a
rather bent and battered black hat,
because she wore it in bed when she was
asleep, to keep the rain off her head.
The roof of her tumbledown house was
a bit leaky.

She also wore an old black dress with lots of patches and a pair of long, stripy stockings. The stripy stockings were very colourful because Fanny had used up all the odd bits of wool knitting them. On her feet she had an old pair of slippers which were supposed to have big blue pom-poms on them, but one of the pom-poms had been chewed up by her old dog, Casserole. Fanny didn't mind about that.

Fanny lived by the village school because she was in charge of it and she taught all the children in the village. The school was a bit tumbledown too, but not in nearly such a bad state as Fanny's home. The paint was peeling off the wood and some of her windows were broken.

Sometimes a villager would offer to

mend the windows for her, but Fanny just laughed. 'I couldn't have that window mended! That's where the crows fly in and out. And the old grey squirrel uses that hole when he goes off looking for nuts. Poor thing – he can't climb so well as he used to. You know what old age is!'

Fanny's house was alive with animals of all sizes. There were any number of mice families living upstairs and downstairs. There were bats in the bathroom and badgers in the bedroom. There were foxes in the front room and rabbits in the back room. There were beetles and spiders inside and the walls outside were covered with the little cupped nests of martins and swallows.

All day long, and half the night too, the house chirped and squeaked and twittered, whilst little feet scampered and wings fluttered endlessly. But Fanny didn't mind about that. The

animals were happy, she was happy,
and the children that came to her school
were happy.

Nobody was quite sure what Fanny
taught the children. She was supposed
to teach them reading and writing and
maths and how to find America and
what the highest mountain in the world
was. (It's Mount Everest.)

But instead the children went home
from Fanny Witch's doing very
strange things, like turning toadstools

into frogs. This sometimes made the
villagers cross because they thought it
was more important to know your five
times table. However the children
enjoyed it and they were very fond of
Fanny Witch, even if she did forget to
give them their lunch sometimes. (Fanny
Witch seemed able to forget anything
and everything and she quite often did.)

Then, early one misty morning, a monster came over the big hill. He was almost as big as a giant and he had huge, shining eyes, like green balloons, only bigger. He had a big grinning mouth like a shark, only with fewer teeth. He should have had more teeth than a shark, but a few weeks earlier he had tried to eat a rock and several teeth had got broken.

The awful thing was a Boosnatch, and he didn't just come marching over the hill . . . he came over the hill riding a giant bicycle. It had great big wheels with extra thick tyres and great big pedals and a great big basket on the front of it.

The Boosnatch rode down into the village and because it was all downhill he took his feet off the pedals and stuck them up on his handlebars and swished down into the silent village. He thought he was very clever indeed. When he got into the village he propped his bicycle up against a tree and then he went and stood in Jessica's back garden and waited.

An alarm clock went off inside the house. People began to get up. The Boosnatch grinned and licked his lips. Jessica's family came downstairs to breakfast. Just as she was about to pour out her cereal, the Boosnatch poked a big hairy hand round the back door and shouted:

BOO! Everybody fell of their chairs with horror. All except Jessica, who had been snatched up by the monster and popped into a sack. Then he went tramping off to Daniel's house.

Daniel was out in the garden, stirring
the frogspawn with a stick, to see if it
would hatch more quickly. (It
wouldn't.) The Boosnatch peered over
the roof at him, reached down
and – BOO! Into the sack went Daniel
and off marched the Boosnatch
humming cheerfully to himself.

When he got to Max's house he
stopped. Max was just getting out of the
bath and wrapping a towel round
himself when a huge hairy hand with
wriggly fingers came in through the
bathroom window and –
BOO! Max gave a squeak and was
popped into the sack.

And so the Boosnatch went round the village. He snatched Lorna from her bicycle and Michael from his bed. He got Sarah before she had finished dressing and she had a jumper and pyjama trousers on.

By the time the sack was full the village was wild with alarm. People were rushing up and down the roads, shouting and screaming and calling for help, especially when they saw the size of the Boosnatch. They seized brooms and spades and forks and went running after the monster, trying to get him to drop the sack.

But the Boosnatch laughed loudly and threw the sack carelessly over his shoulder. (That made everybody squeak!) Then he strode out of the village, popped the sack in his bicycle basket, and pedalled off over the hill.

Fanny Witch had not seen any of this.
She had been far too busy digging up
worms for the new family of blackbirds
that had just hatched out in the hallway.
When she finished she thought it must
be time for school and she was
surprised when no children turned up.
She took off her bent black hat and
scratched her hair. A nesting sparrow
flew out angrily. 'Oh! Did I disturb
you? Well, I don't know. I thought it
was Monday, but it must be Sunday
because the children haven't come to
school.'

Really of course it was Thursday, but Fanny was so very forgetful. While she stood on the doorstep wondering what day it was, a big crowd of noisy villagers came hurrying down the road.

'Fanny! Fanny Witch! You must do something! A Boosnatch has come bicycling over the hill and stolen all the children! It's terrible. It's awful! Those poor children!'

'A Boosnatch?' repeated Fanny. 'Are you quite sure? I don't think I've seen a Boosnatch since . . . since – well, certainly not for a very long time.'

'It was definitely a Boosnatch!' cried Jessica's father.

'Hmmm. Did it have eyes like green balloons?'

'Yes!'

'And a mouth like a shark?'

'Yes! Except it had a few teeth missing.'

'Oh dear,' murmured Fanny. 'It does sound just like a Boosnatch. I'd better do something.'

'Please, please do,' cried everybody. 'You are our only hope.'

So Fanny went inside and sat down and began to think very hard. She was worried, because she wasn't too sure how to deal with a Boosnatch. She fetched an enormous book that was covered all over with cobwebs and dust. She opened it at the beginning and hunted right through it until she came to a page headed THE BOOSNATCH.

Fanny Witch bent over the page and read carefully, muttering to herself all the while. 'Hmmm. Is that so! Goodness me! As many teeth as that – would you believe it!' Then she shut the book with a bang that left clouds of dust floating in the little room, and she began to walk round and round thinking very, VERY hard.

Casserole sat in the old rocking chair and watched her until his eyes went all giddy and he barked at her to stop. And the more Fanny went round in circles and the more she tried to think, the more she couldn't think of anything at all. At last she fell exhausted on to the old sofa and started snoring.

Casserole fetched his blanket from his basket and tugged it over Fanny's legs to keep her warm. He curled himself across her feet, and soon his whiskers were twitching with dreams about rabbits and sticks and giant bones.

Fanny Witch had a dream too. She
dreamed she was walking through a
wood and there were hundreds of birds
singing – suddenly they all stopped.
Fanny felt she was being stared at. She
glanced round – nothing! She turned
again – nothing! But she was almost
sure she heard somebody whisper Boo!
She took another step and all at once the
ground vanished from beneath her and
she fell head first into a huge hole. Her
big black dress blossomed around her
like a parachute and down she floated to
the bottom of the deep, dark hole.

She gazed back at the top, so very far
away and suddenly a horrible, hairy
face appeared at the edge, grinning at
her and showing lots of teeth.

'Help!' yelled Fanny, and she woke herself up. She had fallen off the sofa and Casserole was standing over her, licking her face. 'Oh! It's you, Casserole. I thought it was the Boosnatch.'

Casserole was quite upset at being called a Boosnatch and he stopped licking Fanny at once. Fanny didn't notice. She got to her feet, pulled her hat firmly on top of her head and gave the dog a big smile.

'Casserole,' she said, 'we are going to dig a pit.'

Fanny went straight outside and
began work at once. She dug and dug
and dug. It was hard work and made

her feel hot, so first of all she rolled up
her sleeves and then she tucked her dress
into her knickers. And she dug and
dug and dug. 'Soon be done,' she said
to Casserole, who was very busy with
his front paws too. 'And when it's done,
the Boosnatch will fall into it and we
shall have him!'

Fanny dug half the pit before she realised that she could use magic to do all the hard work for her. She climbed out of the hole, waved her wand and cried – 'Ikky spikky spoo!' Then the rusty old spade dug all by itself, sending fountains of earth shooting up in the air, and in a moment the work was done.

'I think that is quite deep enough,' said Fanny, looking over the edge. 'It must be deeper than the Boosnatch, or he will be able to climb out. I'm not sure how tall a Boosnatch is, but he can't be so tall that he could escape from THIS pit!'

Then Fanny Witch put the spade back in the garden shed and went inside. She made herself a pot of tea and some bread and jam. She put some supper down for Casserole, and when she had finished she set her alarm clock for nice and early in the morning and she went to bed.

Early next day Fanny went out to the
big pit. She covered over the edge with
lots of branches and leaves, and she told

Casserole to wait at the house. 'I'm going to change myself into a little girl,' said Fanny. 'When the Boosnatch sees me he will try to grab me and he will step on to the pit and fall straight into it. Isn't that a good plan?'

Casserole gave a loud bark and ran back to the house with his tail between his legs. He was scared. He didn't like Fanny doing magic and he didn't like Boosnatches, so he hid just behind the front door and only left his nose poking out.

Fanny stood by the pit and shouted 'Ikky Spikky Spoo!' There was a flash and suddenly Fanny was no longer there, but sitting in her place was a sweet little girl with golden hair in bunches and a wonderful blue velvet dress. The only way you could tell it was Fanny was because she still had a nose like a potato, though just a little smaller than normal.

Hardly had the magic change taken place when the Boosnatch came riding down the hill on his bicycle, whistling cheerfully. Fanny Witch waved her arms and cried out to the giant.

'Hallo! Can't catch me! Can't catch me!'

The Boosnatch smiled a big smile. 'Huh huh huh! Oh yes I can!' he said. He jumped off his bicycle and came plodding over to Fanny, waggling his hairy fingers at her.

KERRACK!
KERRUNCH!

The branches gave way and just as the Boosnatch grabbed Fanny he tumbled down into the pit. There was an earth-shaking bump and a cloud of dust rose into the air.

'Ow!' muttered the Boosnatch, rubbing his head. 'That was a big hole.' Then he stood up and looked over the

edge of the pit. Poor Fanny's heart did
cartwheels inside her. She hadn't made
the pit deep enough! It only came up as
high as the Boosnatch's shoulders.

The Boosnatch popped Fanny into his

sack and climbed out as easily as getting out of the bath. Then he flung the sack over his shoulder, (that made Fanny squeak!) and went back to his bicycle.

Casserole came creeping out of the front door of the house and watched. He saw Fanny get caught. He saw the Boosnatch climb out of the pit. He saw the Boosnatch cycle off over the hill. Then he growled angrily and barked and he ran after them dodging from tree to tree and snarling from a safe distance.

By the time the dog had followed
Fanny and the Boosnatch to the giant's
home he was quite worn out. He hid
behind a rock to watch. The Boosnatch
took the sack from his bicycle basket
and carefully opened it. He put in a big
hairy hand and pulled Fanny Witch out.
She sat on his palm, blinking in the
sunlight and decided it was time to
change back to her normal self.

'Ikky Spikky Spoo!' she cried.

'Bless you,' said the Boosnatch.

'I beg your pardon?'

'I thought you sneezed,' said the Boosnatch. 'Would you like a hanky? I've got one here somewhere.' He began to search his pockets.

'I didn't sneeze,' said Fanny, getting all hot and bothered because the spell hadn't worked. 'I was saying a spell.'

The Boosnatch froze and went deathly white. 'A spell?' he whispered. 'Urgh!' And he threw Fanny to the ground as if she were some terribly poisonous spider. 'You're not a witch, are you?' he asked fearfully.

'Yes I am,' said Fanny. 'Ikky spikky spoo!' she repeated. There was a flash and back came the old Fanny, bent hat and all.

But the Boosnatch was trembling all over and crying, with quick little sobs. 'It's rotten. It's a rotten trick to play – pretending to be a nice little girl and all along you were a witch. It's not fair.'

Fanny didn't know what to do. She
shrugged her shoulders, waved her arms
helplessly and went red with
embarrassment. When Casserole saw the
weak state the Boosnatch was in he
trotted out from the rock and growled
bravely at the giant. He even dashed up
and tugged at the giant's shoelaces.

Fanny and Casserole were interrupted
by a shout of joy. 'It's Fanny Witch!
Fanny's here!' The children from the
village came running round them, asking
a hundred questions. 'What are you
doing here? We've been having such fun.'

Fanny was astonished. She thought all the children had been eaten. 'Hasn't the Boosnatch been horrible?' she asked. Little Jessica just burst out laughing and Daniel said he thought the Boosnatch was something Fanny had magicked for them as a surprise. That left Fanny with a lot of explaining to do herself, and by the time she had finished, the Boosnatch was sitting up quite happily, drying his eyes on his shirt tail.

'Does that mean you aren't going to put a spell on me? Aren't you going to turn me into a Groggle?'

'Of course not. I don't even know what a Groggle is,' answered Fanny. 'But why did you take the children?'

The Boosnatch sniffed. 'I was lonely. It seemed so nice down in the village with the children laughing and shouting. I was lonely and cold and wet. It's not much fun living in the open all the time – not when it rains and the leaves

drip all over you. It's even worse in
winter of course. Have you tried
sitting in the snow all day? It's not very
comfortable. Then sometimes it's the
wind, stabbing at your back like a
thousand frozen icicles . . . '

'Stop, stop!' cried Fanny. 'I can't bear listening to any more.' The Boosnatch's sad tale had set all the children sniffling. Even Casserole was lying there with his head drooped over the Boosnatch's left foot, as if he were trying to comfort the poor giant.

Fanny Witch blew her nose. 'I know just what to do,' she declared. 'Come on.'

Then they all set off for the village.

The Boosnatch put everybody,
including Fanny Witch, in his bicycle
basket and off they went, with the
children yelling and screaming as they
went over any bumps. Fanny waved her
hat in the air and Casserole barked and
barked.

That was how they arrived in the village. Daniel's Mum took one look at the speeding bicycle, dropped her washing and screamed.

'The Boosnatch is back! The Boosnatch is back!' She rushed indoors to hide. But as soon as the children jumped out of the basket the villagers knew that everything was all right.

They came out one by one and shook
hands with the Boosnatch – at least the
giant held each villager in his hand and
shook them up and down gently. After
that the villagers began to understand
that the Boosnatch, though very big,
was also very nice.

Later that day Fanny Witch took the giant over to the school and pointed out the old school hall. 'We only use it during the day,' she said. 'I thought you might like to sleep in it at night.'

The Boosnatch's eyes went wide. 'For me?' he stammered. 'A bedroom! A real bedroom for me?' A smile slowly spread across his face until it became a huge grin. Fanny smiled. 'I think I'd better make one or two alterations before you try it.' She thought for a moment and wiggled her fingers at the old hall. 'Ikky spikky spoo!'

A flash of red and a cloud of smoke rose from the roof and slowly drifted away. The Boosnatch stared at the hall very hard. 'It's just the same,' he murmured, with a touch of disappointment.

'You look inside. Go on – lift up the roof.'

The Boosnatch bent down and

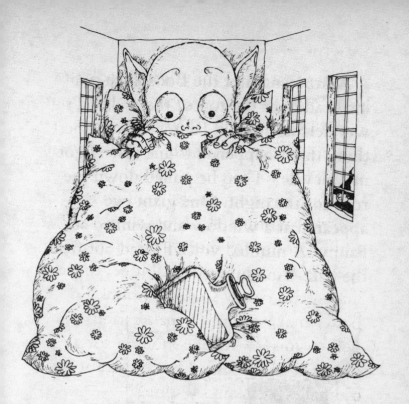

pushed up the roof. He peered inside,
gave a little gasp and stepped into his
new bedroom. Inside was a beautiful,
soft quilt, all puffed and fluffed up like
a marshmallow mountain range. He
snuggled down beneath it and his feet
touched upon something hot and
floppy – he reached down and pulled
out a giant hot water bottle.

A moment later the Boosnatch put his head over the top of the wall. 'It's wonderful,' he told Fanny. 'It's the best thing that's happened to me since I got my bicycle.' Then he pulled down the roof for the night. One giant eye appeared at a window and winked at Fanny. A muffled voice floated out from the hall. 'Goodnight!'

'Goodnight, Boosnatch,' said Fanny,
and she went to her little cottage. It was
her own bed time. The birds in the roof
were chirping very quietly and the
foxes and badgers had already gone out
for the night. Fanny lay back in bed and
listened. A very strange noise came to
her ears. It sounded just like an old car
trying to start itself, over and over
again. Most peculiar. Then she smiled.
Of course, it was the Boosnatch
snoring.

Fanny laughed. She had birds in the roof, bats in the bathroom, badgers in the bedroom and a giant Boosnatch in

the school hall. She turned over and went to sleep. Beneath the bed Casserole was dreaming about going for another ride in the Boosnatch's bicycle basket.

Some other Young Puffins

RADIO RESCUE

John Escott

Mia is enjoying her holiday with her father by the seaside, away from her mother who is always criticizing her for not reading and writing well. But Mia's reading difficulties lead her into all sorts of trouble when she ignores the Danger sign.

MICHAEL AND THE JUMBLE-SALE CAT

Marjorie Newman

Michael lives in the children's home with his best friend Lee and his precious jumble-sale cat. One day Jenny, his social worker, asks if he'd like to live with a new family and Michael is thrown into confusion, but when the day arrives for him to leave the children's home he is both sad and glad. His new family turn out to be very special indeed!

ANOTHER BIG STORY BOOK

Richard Bamberger

One of the foremost experts of literature for children has collected here some of the world's most enchanting and magical fairy tales. From the English tale 'Jack and the Beanstalk' to the Indian 'Wali Dad the Simple', these are stories parents will enjoy telling and children will remember with pleasure for the rest of their lives.

THE WIZARD PARTY

Thelma Lambert

Three stories about the lovable Benny and his mad schemes, which never turn out as planned. For instance, he decides to have his own Hallowe'en party when his friend's party is cancelled, but in spite of careful planning his Dad has to come to the rescue when things start to go wrong.

JAMES AND THE TV STAR

Michael Hardcastle

Two entertaining stories about Katie and James's clever ideas. James has an idea about how to meet his TV hero, and Katie is having a birthday party on the same day as her friend's . . .

BURNT SAUSAGES AND CUSTARD

Marjorie Newman

The twins are sad when Mum says a picnic in the park will have to do for their birthday, but when the day arrives it turns out to be full of surprises and very special indeed!

BELLA'S DRAGON

Chris Powling

Two fantastic stories about ordinary children. In the first, Bella is surprised to see a dragon flop down into her back garden. School is closed and she's bored – what could be more fun than to help a lonely dragon find a new den? In the second story, Frankie makes a huge mistake when he meets a witch stuck in a ditch and gives her back her magic wand.

THE RAILWAY CAT AND THE HORSE

Phyllis Arkle

Alfie and his friends are very curious to learn that a valuable horse is going to be delivered to their station. Could it be a racehorse, they wonder? They soon find out that it's no ordinary horse, but one that's going to need very special treatment!

THE HODGEHEG

Dick King-Smith

The story of Max the hedgehog who become a hodgeheg, who becomes a hero. The hedgehog family of Number 5A are a happy bunch but they dream of reaching the Park. Unfortunately, a very busy road lies between them and their goal and no one has found a way to cross it in safety. No one, that is, until the determined young Max decides to solve the problem once and for all . . .

HELP!

Margaret Gordon

Fred and Flo are very helpful little pigs. The problem is, the more helpful they try to be, the more trouble they cause. Whether they are washing Grandad's car, looking after Baby or doing the decorating, disaster is never far away! Four hilarious stories featuring two very charming – and helpful – piglets.

DUMBELLINA

Brough Girling

What could be worse than the thought of moving house, changing school and leaving all your friends behind? When her Mum announces they are moving, Rebecca feels totally miserable – until she meets Dumbellina, the iron fairy.

ENOUGH IS ENOUGH

Margaret Nash

Usually when Miss Boswell uses her magic phrase, it works: Class 1 know that she means enough is *enough*, and get back to work, for a while at least. But when Miss Boswell's special plant begins to grow and grow until it has wiped the sums off the board, curling right out of the classroom and is heading for the kitchen, not even shouting 'Enough is enough!' will stop it!

DUSTBIN CHARLIE

Ann Pilling

Charlie had always liked seeing what people threw out in their dustbins. So he's thrilled to find the toy of his dreams among the rubbish in the skip. But during the night, someone else takes it. The culprit in this highly enjoyable story turns out to be the most surprising person.

CLASS THREE AND THE BEANSTALK

Martin Waddell

Two unusual stories which will amaze you. Class Three's project on growing things gets out of hand after they plant a packet of Jackson's Giant Bean seeds. And when Wilbur Small is coming home, the whole street is buzzing – except for Tom Grice and his family, who are new in the street so don't know what the fuss is about, or why people are so nervous!

THE TWIG THING

Jan Mark

As soon as Rosie and Ella saw the house they knew that something was missing. It had lots of windows and stairs, but where was the garden? When they move in, they find a twig thing which they put in water on the window-sill, and gradually things begin to change.

DODIE

Finola Akister

Dodie the dachshund lives with Miss Smith and Tigercat in a country cottage. He has all sorts of adventures, because he's a very special dog. He is very good at finding things. He finds Miss Smith's key when she gets locked out, he finds Tigercat's new kitten, and he even finds a prickly hedgehog! Life is never dull for Dodie.

HERE COME THE TWINS

Beverly Cleary

Twins are full of surprises: just ask Mr Lemon, the postman. Janet and Jimmy can turn anything into a game, whether it's getting their first grown-up beds, or going to buy new shoes. But what will they do when their next-door neighbour gives them each a dog biscuit? Give them to a dog? No, that would be too easy!

THE FRIDAY PARCEL

Ann Pilling

Two highly enjoyable stories in which Matt goes to stay on his own with Gran-in-the-country, and sets his heart on buying a lion at the jungle sale.

STICK TO IT, CHARLIE

Joy Allen

In these two 'Charlie' adventures, Charlie meets a new friend and finds a new interest – playing the piano. The new friend proves his worth when Charlie and the gang find themselves in a tight spot. As for the piano – well, even football comes second place!

THE LITTLE EXPLORER

Margaret Joy

The little explorer is setting out on a long voyage. He is going in search of the pinkafrillia, the rarest flower in the world. Together with Knots, the sailor, and Peckish, the Parrot, Stanley journeys through the jungle of Allegria – and what adventures they have!

THE SCHOOL POOL GANG

Geraldine Kaye

Billy is the head of the Back Lane Gang and he's always coming up with good ideas. So when money is needed for a new school pool, his first idea is to change the gang's name. His next idea – to raise money by giving donkey rides – leads to all sorts of unexpected and exciting happenings!